Usborne Engli
Level

The Elves and the Shoemaker

Retold by Laura Cowan

Illustrated by Olga Demidova

English language consultant: Peter Viney

Contents

You can listen to the story online here:
www.usborneenglishreaders.com/
elvesandtheshoemaker

In a small town, long ago, there lived an old man and his wife. The old man made shoes in a little workshop, and his wife helped him.

The old man was a good shoemaker,
but the winters were difficult for him.
His hands were always cold, so he worked
very slowly.

He couldn't make many shoes. Often
he and his wife had no money, and only a
little bread to eat.

One night, the shoemaker said to his wife, "This is my last piece of leather. It's just enough for one more pair of shoes."

"Well, you must make them, and I hope we can sell them," his wife said.

Before he went to bed, the shoemaker cut the leather into pieces. He left the pieces on his work table. "It's very late. I can finish these in the morning," he said.

The bright winter sun woke the shoemaker early. He got up and went downstairs. The pieces of leather weren't there! On the work table was a new pair of shoes.

They had tiny, strong stitches, and they were beautiful. The old man didn't understand.

He called to his wife. "Look! Did you
do this?"

His wife came downstairs and saw
the shoes. "No, I didn't. I can't sew tiny
stitches like that!"

"Who can? *I* can't," said the shoemaker.
"Maybe it's magic."

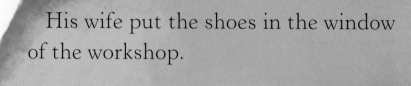

His wife put the shoes in the window of the workshop.

Later that morning, a stranger in an expensive suit and hat came in and bought them. "What wonderful shoes!" he said to the shoemaker, "Everyone in the city is going to want a pair. I must come here again." He paid the shoemaker a lot of money.

The shoemaker and his wife were very happy. With the money, they bought some food and had a good hot meal. The shoemaker also bought enough leather for two more pairs of shoes.

That evening, he cut out all the pieces and left them on the work table.

"I have lots of work for tomorrow now," he said, and went to bed.

In the morning, he came downstairs. On the work table there were two new pairs of shoes, one pink and one green. They were even better than the first pair.

"I *know* this is magic," said the shoemaker, and he called to his wife.

She came downstairs. "Someone is helping us," she said, "but who? Well, let's put the shoes in the window."

That afternoon, the rich stranger came back with two friends, and his friends bought both pairs.

The shoemaker and his wife had enough money for some new clothes, and they bought enough leather for four pairs of shoes.

The same thing happened again that night. In the evening, the shoemaker cut out the leather pieces, and in the morning there were four beautiful pairs of shoes on the work table. All the pairs were different.

One pair was pretty and pink, with neat white stitches. One was dark blue, perfect for a party. There was a pair of tiny red shoes for a child, and a pair of strong black boots.

The rich man's friends bought them all, and soon everyone was talking about the old man's workshop. Everyone wanted a pair of his wonderful shoes.

One evening, his wife said, "Who is making these lovely shoes? Don't you want to know?"

The shoemaker said, "Of course I do, but how *can* we know?"

"I have an idea," said his wife.

That evening, they didn't go to bed. They hid behind some coats at the back of the workshop and waited. Finally, in the middle of the night, the door opened a little.

Two tiny men danced in. Their clothes were just rags.

They climbed onto the table, picked up the pieces of leather and started working.

The little men worked fast. One sewed quickly and neatly, and the other one hammered.

Before the sun came up, there were ten pairs of shoes on the table. Then the men climbed down to the floor and ran out of the shop.

The shoemaker and his wife came and looked at the shoes. They were red, blue, pink, yellow, white, black, green, brown, silver and gold.

Some were for women, some were for men and some were for little children. There were shoes for work and shoes for parties. Every pair had the same perfect tiny stitches.

"Well, well," said the shoemaker's wife, "Our secret helpers are elves!"

"Elves!" said the shoemaker. "I don't believe it!"

"We're rich because of those elves," his wife said, "We must say thank you."

"How can we do that?" asked the shoemaker.

"*I* know," his wife smiled. "Those poor little men were wearing rags. I can do something about that."

She found some old clothes and cut them into pieces. Then she started sewing. Before evening there were two tiny coats, two tiny shirts and two tiny suits.

Finally the shoemaker made two tiny pairs of shoes. "What a good idea! They're the perfect present," he said.

That night, the shoemaker and his wife left the new clothes on the table. Then they hid under the coats again and waited. Again the door opened a little, and the tiny men danced in.

Suddenly they saw their presents on the table.

They put the clothes on and danced around the room. Their eyes were bright. "Look! Nobody ever gave us clothes before," said one elf. "Don't we look smart!"

"All the elves are going to want clothes like these!" laughed the other. Then they danced out of the shop.

After that, the elves never came back. The shoemaker sewed and hammered, and made more beautiful shoes. They weren't like the elves' shoes, but it didn't matter. Lots of people wanted to buy them anyway.

Soon the shoemaker and his wife left their small town and found a smart new workshop in the city. They lived there for many years, and they were never poor or hungry again.

One cold winter afternoon, the shoemaker's wife stopped suddenly outside another workshop. She looked through the window.

"What a beautiful hat!" she said, "And what tiny, neat stitches. I know those stitches – they're elves' stitches!"

About the story

Jacob and Wilhelm Grimm were brothers. They lived in Germany two hundred years ago. Together, they collected and told lots of stories, like *Hansel and Gretel*, *Little Red Riding Hood* and *Snow White*.

The Grimm Brothers told a few stories about elves, but *The Elves and the Shoemaker* is the most famous. In lots of other Grimm stories, there is one really bad person. *The Elves and the Shoemaker* is different because everyone in the story is nice, and the story is about kindness.

In 1902, Beatrix Potter wrote *The Tailor of Gloucester* (a tailor makes clothes, and Gloucester is a city in England). In it, the tailor is ill and the mice in his house finish his work at night. Maybe Beatrix Potter was thinking of the elves in this story.

Activities

The answers are on page 32.

Talk about the people in the story

Choose a sentence for each picture.

1.

The elves

2.

The shoemaker and his wife

3.

The stranger and his friends

	B.		C.
Often they have no money.	They buy three pairs of shoes.		Their clothes are just rags.

What happens when?

Can you put these pictures and sentences in order?

A.
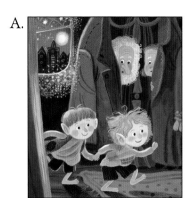
Two tiny men danced in.

B.

"Who is making these lovely shoes?"

C.

On the work table a new pair of shoes

D.

The little men worked fast.

E.

"This is my last piece of leather"

F.

That afternoon, the rich stranger came back with two frien

What do they want?

Choose the right sentence for each person.

B. We want to have a good hot meal.   We want to wear smart clothes.

A. I want to make hats.   B. I want to sell shoes.

The elves   The shoemaker

B. want to say thank you to the elves.   I want to make a new dress.

A. I want to be a shoemaker.   B. I want to buy these wonderful shoes.

The shoemaker's wife   The rich stranger

Wonderful shoes

Choose the right word to finish each sentence.

clean   pretty   dark   ugly

busy   strong   interesting   tiny

1.

...red shoes for a child

2.

...black boots

3.

...and pink with neat stitches

4.

...blue, perfect for a party

What are they saying?

One word in each sentence is wrong.
Can you choose the right word instead?

1.

I help my friend.

husband   stranger   child

2.

I need an idea.

love   have   remember

3.

Nobody ever gave us bags before!

hats   clothes   money

4.

I see those stitches.

know   want   like

Word list

bright (adj) when something gives a lot of light, or is very shiny, it is bright.

call (v) when you call someone, you speak to them in a loud voice, especially when you want them to come to you.

elf, elves (n) tiny magical people in stories.

finally (adv) after a long time.

hammer (v) when you hammer something, you use a hammer (a tool with a wooden handle and a metal head) to hit it into place.

leather (n) leather is often used to make shoes.

neat (adj) very well done, not messy.

pair (n) two of something together, for example shoes or socks.

perfect (adj) if something is perfect, there is nothing wrong with it.

piece (n) a little of something or a small part of something.

rags (n) when cloth is very old and has holes in it, it is called rags.

sew (v) to fix two pieces of cloth together with a needle and thread. You can sew cloth together to make clothes.

shoemaker (n) a person who makes shoes.

smart (adj) if something is smart, it looks good. Smart clothes are clean and well made. People can also look smart.

stitch (n) a loop of thread that holds two pieces of cloth together.

suit (n) two or three pieces of clothing that go together, for example a jacket and trousers (or pants in American English), or a jacket and skirt.

tiny (adj) really small.

workshop (n) a place where someone makes things.

Answers

Talk about the people in the story
1. C
2. A
3. B

What happens when?
E, C, F, B, A, D

What do they want?
B, B, A, B

Wonderful shoes
1. tiny
2. strong
3. pretty
4. dark

What are they saying?
1. ~~friend~~ husband
2. ~~need~~ have
3. ~~bags~~ clothes
4. ~~see~~ know

You can find information about other Usborne English Readers here: www.usborneenglishreaders.com

Designed by Sam Whibley

Series designer: Laura Nelson Norris

Edited by Mairi Mackinnon

Digital imaging: Nick Wakeford

Page 24: picture of the Brothers Grimm © Fine Art Images/Heritage Images via Getty Images
Illustration *The Tailor Mouse* by Beatrix Potter (1886-1943) © Tate London, 2018

First published in 2019 by Usborne Publishing Ltd.,
Usborne House, 83-85 Saffron Hill, London EC1N 8RT, England.
www.usborne.com Copyright © 2019 Usborne Publishing Ltd.